THE MEMORY BOOK

A Grandparent's Guide to Preserving Your Family's Precious Heritage

Editor: Mike Martin
Contributing Editor: Clancy Strock
Assistant Editors: Mike Beno, Kristine Krueger, Henry de Fiebre
Art Director: Greg Miller
Art Associate: Sue Myers
Photo Coordination: Trudi Bellin
Production Assistant: Judy Pope
Publisher: Roy J. Reiman

International Standard Book Number: 0-89821-159-X
Library of Congress Catalog Number: 95-73094
All rights reserved. Printed in U.S.A.
Cover Photo: Robert C. Dawson/F-Stock
Back Cover Photo: Dianne Dietrich Leis

© 1996 Reiman Publications, L.P., 5400 S. 60th St., Greendale WI 53129

For additional copies of this book or information on other books, write: Reminisce Books, P.O. Box 990, Greendale WI 53129.

CONTENTS

- ⑦ Where Your Family Came From
- ⑮ When You Were Little
- ㉕ Chores and School
- ㉟ Tales Worth Telling
- ㊶ Leaving Home
- ㊾ Marriage and Work
- ㊼ Raising a Family
- ㊻ Family Traditions
- ㊽ One More Look Back... And a Look Ahead

Some Helpful Hints for Preserving Your Family's Precious Heritage

By Clancy Strock, Contributing Editor, Reminisce

GRANDFATHER STEVENS was a wonderful storyteller. If the weather was nice, he and I would walk a few blocks to sit beside the Rock River, where he'd tell me about his life.

He actually remembered a man racing past his boyhood home, shouting that the Civil War had ended. He told tales about working for the railroad and how he'd played chess by telegraph with other stationmasters on the line. Oh, so many rich and wonderful stories!

Today, I'm a grandfather and it's my turn to pass along the family legends and history. But the grandchildren all live hundreds of miles away, so we don't have much time together.

Recently my oldest grandchild phoned. Tim, 27, said he didn't know much about the Strock family. Could we just sit down somewhere for a day or two so I could fill in some of the blanks? He's at an age when roots and heritage are becoming of interest.

And 14-year-old grandson Andrew shows curiosity about what school was like when I was a boy. What did I do for fun in those pre-TV, pre-Nintendo days? What sort of jobs did I have? What was life like during the Great Depression?

Memories for the Children

Ernest Webber, a *Reminisce* reader, did what we all should do, but probably won't. He put his life's story into what became a 300-page book, *Growing Up in the Ozarks*.

"I wrote it, first, for my children," he says. And what a treasure it is, not only for Ernest's children but for future generations of his family.

Let's face it, not many of us will write our own book. But what you hold in your hands will let you come close.

On the following pages, you'll find dozens of questions designed to *prompt* you…to get you thinking about the important times in your life. They're sure to help you recall some of your most treasured family memories that need to be recorded.

Complete these chapters, and you'll end up with a detailed one-of-a-kind family history. What a wonderful gift to pass along to the young ones in your family and all the generations that will follow!

If some of the questions don't jog a memory at first, just skip along to the next. Don't try to tackle all the questions in one sitting. That would turn a fun project into hard work. Instead, answer one or two questions per evening. That way, this memory-preserving project just may become the highlight of your day.

Get the Family Involved

After you've filled in the questions, you'll probably want to go further. You'll discover (as I did) that your personal history can be richer and more complete if you get together with others in your family who can contribute their own memories.

"Remember the time when Mom and Dad took us to…?" "I'll never forget the day when you…" "The best time that I ever had was…"

If you can, use a tape recorder while everyone shares their tales. It's a lot easier than taking notes. Some people even use a camcorder.

How I wish I could pop a video cassette into the VCR and bring back Grampa and Gramma Stevens on my TV screen. Wouldn't it be something if the little ones could actually see and hear their great-great-grandparents and listen as they recall their lives?

Don't forget to dig out family scrapbooks to help prompt some memories, too. Mom was a diligent scrapbook-keeper. There are ticket stubs from concerts, the 1924 hospital bill from when I was born (10 days, $88!), wedding announcements, newspaper clippings, the first letter I sent during my first trip away from home—every single one an important memory-jogger.

Just as important as the family legends are family photo albums. There you are at age 6, arm around "Laddie", the faithful collie who followed you everywhere. There's the family reunion picture around the picnic table one Fourth of July…your first car…Jimmy in his high school graduation cap and gown…

Put Names with Faces

They're all wonderful memories to you, but remember that none of the subjects in these photos will mean a thing to future generations if the folks in the photos aren't identified!

Don't wait a day longer to clearly write down the identity of the people in your photos. Our Strock family Bible has a whole section of faded daguerreotypes and early-day photos of my ancestors. But there isn't a name on a single one! Their identity is lost forever.

What I've done with my keepsake photos is turn them over and *lightly and very carefully* write down the names of everyone in each photo, as well as where they're perched on the family tree.

For instance: "Howard Strock, uncle, and son of Homer and Amanda." When possible, I date the picture.

Does all this sound like a lot of work? Maybe. But the payoff can be grand.

Two years ago, for example, I spent 3 long months going through thousands of feet of home movies that covered my children's growing-up years.

I worked at it nights, weekends and any other spare time I could find. My eyes burned from squinting, my back ached from bending over the film viewer and there were times when I felt like quitting.

I ended up with an hour of film, which was transferred to videotape. A copy went to each of the kids. Every year or so, they show it to their kids. "Here's me, growing up in our family." Someday those kids can show it to *their* kids. "See, there's Grampa when he was growing up."

Was it work? Not at all. Just pure joy (along with more than a few happy tears).

So, why not turn the page and get started? We at *Reminisce* wish you much joy.

Where Your Family Came From

From what part of the world did your family emigrate? _____

_____
_____
_____
_____
_____
_____
_____

Did an older relative ever relate the story of that journey? _____

_____
_____
_____
_____
_____
_____
_____

> UNLESS you tell them, your grandchildren will likely never get the opportunity to know your parents and grandparents. Here's your chance to tell them about those important people—and your family's oldest known relatives.

When was this and where did your ancestors settle?

Do you know why they ended up in that particular part of the country?

How far back can you trace your family tree?

Do you have any relatives who were famous—or who took part in well-known historical incidents? _____

_____

_____

_____

_____

_____

_____

_____

_____

What were your grandparents' names? _____

_____

_____

_____

Where and when were they born? _____

_____

_____

_____

_____

_____

_____

When you think of your grandparents, what are the strongest images that come to mind?

What was the most enjoyable time you ever spent with your grandmother?

What was the most enjoyable time you ever spent with your grandfather? _____

Can you recall a favorite story either of your grandparents may have told you? _____

What were your parents' full names?

Where and when were your parents born?

Did they ever tell you the story of how they met?

What is the most vivid image of your father from your childhood? _____

_____

What was your mother's maiden name and what do you remember most about her from your childhood? _____

What work did your parents do and what traits do you value most about them as you look back now?

What is the most enjoyable memory you have of time spent with your parents?

What are some of the most valuable lessons taught you by your parents?

When You Were Little

When were you born? _____

_____

_____

_____

Where were you born? _____

_____

_____

_____

Were there any unusual events or circumstances surrounding your birth?

_____

_____

_____

> BACK in the days when you were raised, youngsters grew up in a different world than they do now. In this chapter, you can share your earliest memories of the days before television, home videos and personal computers.

_____

_____

_____

_____

Do you know how your name was chosen?

What is the earliest memory you can recall?

Are there any funny baby stories about you that your family shared? _____

What kind of baby were you? _____

Did your parents ever relate any special difficulties they had when you were a baby? _____

Were you colicky?

At first, did you sleep through the night?

Did you have a favorite toy?

What was your favorite food?

How many brothers and sisters did you have? (Please list them in the order they were born, including dates if you can remember them.) _____

_____

_____

_____

_____

_____

_____

_____

Where did you fit in? _____

_____

_____

_____

_____

Did you have a nickname? _____

_____

How about the other members of your family? _____

_____

_____

_____

_____

What do you remember most about the house (or houses) where you grew up?

What was the most mischievous thing you ever did as a young child? _____
_____
_____
_____
_____
_____
_____
_____
_____
_____
_____
_____
_____
_____
_____

Which of your siblings did you get along with the best? _____
_____
_____
_____

Why? _____
_____
_____
_____
_____
_____

The worst? _____
_____
_____
_____

Why? _____
_____
_____
_____
_____

Any memorable stories about a brother or sister come to mind? _____
_____
_____
_____
_____
_____
_____
_____
_____
_____
_____
_____
_____
_____

Did you and your siblings ever pull some prank that you were very glad your parents never learned of? _____
_____
_____
_____
_____
_____

Can you remember what you wanted to be when you grew up?
_____
_____
_____
_____
_____
_____
_____

What was your favorite toy or game when you were small? _____
_____
_____
_____

What was your favorite book? _____
_____
_____

What was your favorite movie? _____
_____

Did you have a favorite pet? _____

_____

_____

Can you remember its name? _____

_____

_____

What do you remember most about your favorite pet (or pets)? _____

_____

_____

_____

_____

_____

_____

_____

_____

_____

_____

Chapter 3

Chores and School

Were you responsible for any household chores? _____

What were they? _____

Which chore did you dislike the most? _____

> FOR most kids, being assigned a family chore is the first taste of responsibility. Here's an opportunity to record what that was like for you— as well as your most vivid recollections of grammar school and high school.

Did you ever get in trouble for not doing it? _____

Did you get an allowance? _____

If so, how much did you get and what kinds of things would you spend it on? _____

When you were growing up, what could you buy for a penny? _____

A nickel? _____

A dime? _____

Was money ever tight in your family when you were growing up? _____

If so, what kinds of things did you and other family members do to help out or get by?
_____
_____
_____
_____
_____
_____

Can you recall how you felt on your first day of school? _____
_____
_____
_____
_____
_____
_____
_____

Where did you go to grammar school? _____
_____
_____

How did you usually get there? _____
_____
_____

Who were your best friends during grammar school?

Why did you get along well with them?

What games did you play at recess?

Which subjects did you like the most? _____

_____

_____

_____

_____

_____

_____

The least? _____

_____

_____

_____

_____

_____

_____

_____

Why? _____

_____

_____

_____

_____

_____

_____

_____

_____

_____

_____

_____

Did you ever miss a long stretch of school due to illness? _____
_____
_____
_____

If so, what did you do to occupy your time while you were housebound? _____
_____
_____
_____

What did you do during summer vacations? _____
_____
_____
_____
_____
_____
_____
_____
_____
_____
_____
_____

What was the most enjoyable time you had during high school? _____

_____
_____
_____
_____
_____
_____
_____
_____

During your high school years, were you involved in sports? _____

_____
_____
_____
_____
_____
_____
_____

If so, what were some of the highlights—and lowlights—of your athletic endeavors? _____

_____
_____
_____
_____
_____
_____
_____

Were you involved in music in school? If so, how? _____
_____
_____
_____
_____
_____
_____
_____

Did you play music into adulthood? _____
_____
_____
_____
_____
_____

Whether or not you ever played, what styles of music have you enjoyed most? _____
_____
_____
_____
_____

What was your favorite song in high school? _____
_____
_____
_____

In later years? _____
_____
_____

What slang words did you use as a teen? Explain how you'd use these terms.

Did you date during high school?

If so, can you recall your first date?

How did it go?

Can you recall what songs or dances were popular when you were in your teens?

What were some of your favorite radio programs? _____

_____

_____

_____

_____

_____

_____

What was the funniest thing you ever witnessed in school? _____

_____

_____

_____

_____

_____

_____

_____

_____

What was your proudest achievement in school? _____

_____

_____

_____

_____

_____

_____

_____

_____

Chapter 4

Tales Worth Telling

Can you briefly tell one or more of your family's best stories or "tall tales"?

> EVERY family has its share of stories that are just too good not to repeat. In this chapter, you can ensure that succeeding generations will continue to enjoy the family wit and wisdom that's their heritage.

Do you recall any family members who were real "characters"?

What was it that earned them their reputation?

Can you recall a favorite story about any of those persons? _____

Can you think of any personal traits or characteristics that seem to "run in the family"?

Did either of your parents have a favorite story they liked to share with you? _____

Can you tell a story about your "worst winter ever"? _____

How about your "hottest summer"? _____

Do you have a favorite story you shared with your children?

Did you ever experience a "blessing in disguise"? Please share the story.

Is there any enduring piece of advice or wisdom that's been passed down from generation to generation in your family? _____

If not, what's the best piece of advice you've ever benefited from? _____

CHAPTER 5

Leaving Home

How old were you when you left home? _____

Where and why did you move out? _____

> IT'S always a big step when a child leaves the security of home. Please share your recollections of young adulthood and what it was like to be "out on your own" in a world very different from the one young people face today.

How did it feel to be on your own for the first time? _____

_____
_____
_____
_____
_____
_____
_____
_____
_____
_____

What were your hopes and dreams for your life when you first went out into the world?

_____
_____
_____
_____
_____
_____
_____
_____
_____
_____
_____
_____

What was your first job after you left home? _____

_____

_____

_____

_____

_____

_____

_____

_____

_____

_____

_____

_____

How did you get it? _____

_____

_____

_____

Who was your boss and how did you get along with him or her? _____

_____

_____

_____

Do you recall how much you were paid? _____

_____

_____

_____

What do you remember most about your first car? _____

How was driving your first car different from driving today? _____

Can you recall the first extended trip (or a particularly memorable trip) you took in your own car? Tell about it. _____

Did you ever go for Sunday drives? Where would you go? With whom? _____

Did you ever ride in a rumble seat? If so, please describe the experience.

How and where did you meet your spouse?

What was your first impression?

What first attracted you to your spouse?

What kinds of entertainment did you two enjoy while you were dating?

How long did the courtship last?

What do you recall about the marriage proposal?

When and where did it happen?

Can you recall your parents' reaction when they learned that you intended to get married?

What do you remember about the planning for your marriage?

CHAPTER 6

Marriage and Work

What was the date of your marriage? _____

What things about your wedding do you remember most vividly? _____

FINDING a mate and building a life together are two of the most fulfilling aspects in many people's lives. Here's a chance to recall your marriage and those exciting days when your new life was beginning to blossom.

How old were each of you when you married? _____

What did you wear on your wedding day? _____

What was the weather like? _____

What was the most memorable wedding gift you received? _____
_____
_____
_____
_____

Can you describe your wedding cake? _____
_____
_____
_____

Did you go on a honeymoon? _____
_____

If so, where? And why was it chosen? _____
_____
_____
_____
_____
_____
_____

How did you get there? _____
_____
_____
_____
_____

What do you remember most about the first house or apartment you lived in after you were married? _____

_____

_____

_____

_____

_____

_____

_____

_____

_____

_____

How did the two of you plan to support yourselves? _____

_____

_____

_____

_____

_____

_____

_____

_____

_____

_____

_____

After living together for a time, what surprised you most about your spouse?

Every couple has a few disagreements. If the two of you did, what were they usually about?

Please tell your favorite story about your mate.

If you were asked to describe your spouse for future generations, what would you want them to know about him or her?

What was the most satisfying job you ever had?

And the least satisfying? _____

Why? _____

Did you or anyone in your family ever serve in the armed forces and/or fight in a war?

What places did you, or another in the family, get sent while serving our country?

What do you remember most about the military?

CHAPTER 7

Raising a Family

When was your first child born? _____

Where was that? _____

Please describe the emotions you felt that day. _____

> **THE THRILL** of becoming a parent is an unforgettable experience. Here's an opportunity to recall the joys of starting your own "brood"—and of learning and growing together as a family.

How did your spouse and/or other relatives react?

Who did your firstborn most closely resemble?

How about your other children? Please list their birth dates in order.

Do any stories come to mind when you carefully think back on their births?

As you raised your family, did you ever move? If so, list the places, in order, you moved to. Note the year for each move, if you can. _____

_____
_____
_____
_____
_____
_____
_____
_____
_____
_____
_____
_____
_____
_____
_____
_____
_____
_____
_____

Which house was your favorite? _____
_____
_____
_____

What did you like most about each house? Why?

What did you like least? Why?

As your children were growing up, what were some of the family hardships you faced together? _____

What lessons do you think those hardships taught? _____

What were some of the more enjoyable activities you did together as a family? _____

What were some of the family rules you made sure your children followed? _____

What's the most important lesson you hope your children learned from you?

Did your children ever do anything that prompted you to say, "Just wait until you have children of your own!"?

Chapter 8

Family Traditions

When you were growing up, were there some customs your family routinely followed on Sundays? _____

> **EVERY FAMILY** develops its own unique way of doing things, whether it's celebrating a birthday or holiday—or just going to church on Sunday. Now is the time to record those special customs for posterity.

What church did you attend? _____

Where would the family get together to celebrate the following holidays, and what special traditions were followed?

Christmas _____

Easter _____

Thanksgiving

Fourth of July

New Year's

Halloween

What were some of the traditional family foods usually prepared for family gatherings?

What is your favorite recipe from among those foods? (Please write it here if you can remember it.) ⎯⎯⎯⎯⎯⎯⎯⎯⎯⎯⎯⎯

⎯⎯

How did you celebrate your birthday as a child? _____

What was the best birthday you ever had? _____

The best gift you ever got? _____

What family heirlooms have been passed down from generation to generation? _____

Which is most important to you? Why? _____

Were you or your family members involved in any annual community activities? _____

What family or holiday tradition would you say has been the most meaningful for you?

Why?

Chapter 9

One More Look Back...and a Look Ahead

What would you say was the funniest thing that's ever happened to you?

> REFLECTING on the past is a great way to put your life into perspective. Here's a chance to look at the most vivid and lasting memories you have—memories that can offer your loved ones some guidance for the future.

Looking back, what has been your favorite time of life? _____

Why? _____

Which person most influenced your life, and why? _____

If you did any traveling, which places did you find most interesting and why. Please note when you traveled there, and with whom.

What have been one or two of the most important things you've learned in your life?

_____
_____
_____
_____
_____
_____
_____
_____
_____
_____

Have you ever made a sacrifice that's made a lasting impression on you? _____

_____
_____
_____
_____
_____
_____
_____
_____
_____
_____

What one thing have you done that's made you most proud? _____

_____
_____
_____
_____
_____
_____
_____
_____
_____
_____
_____
_____
_____
_____

What was the most embarrassing moment of your life? _____

_____
_____
_____
_____
_____
_____
_____
_____
_____
_____
_____
_____
_____
_____

What was the wisest decision you've ever made? _____

_____

_____
_____
_____
_____
_____
_____
_____

_____
_____

Remember a not-so-wise decision? _____

_____
_____
_____
_____
_____
_____
_____
_____
_____
_____
_____
_____

Every family experiences tragedy at one time or another. What is the saddest or most difficult time you've lived through? _____

In times of trouble, who or what has helped pull you through? _____

Who are (or were) your closest friends? _____

What was most special about them? _____

Of all the changes you've seen in the world over the years, which ones do you like the best?

The least?

What makes your family truly unique from other families?

If you had one piece of advice to leave for your children and grandchildren, what would it be?